Stories by Contemporary Writers from Shanghai

THE
MESSENGER'S
LETTER

This book is edited and designed by the Editorial Committee of *Cultural China* series

Managing Directors: Wang Youbu, Xu Naiqing
Editorial Director: Wu Ying
Series Editor: Wang Jiren
Editor: David Specchio

Text by Sun Ganlu
Translation by Daniel Clutton, Gina Wang, He Jing

Interior and Cover Design: Wang Wei
Cover Image: Getty Images

ISBN: 978-1-60220-222-1

Address any comments about *The Messenger's Letter* to:

Better Link Press
99 Park Ave
New York, NY 10016
USA
or
Shanghai Press and Publishing Development Company
F 7 Donghu Road, Shanghai, China (200031)
Email: comments_betterlinkpress@hotmail.com

Printed in China by Shanghai Donnelley Printing Co. Ltd.

1 2 3 4 5 6 7 8 9 10

THE MESSENGER'S LETTER

By Sun Ganlu

Better Link Press

Preface

English readers will be presented with a set of 12 pocket books. These books contain outstanding novellas written by 12 writers from Shanghai over the past 30 years. Most of the writers were born in Shanghai from the late 1940's to the late 1950's. They started their literary careers during or after the 1980's. For various reasons, most of them lived and worked in the lowest social strata in other cities or in rural areas for much of their adult lives. As a result they saw much of the world and learned lessons from real life before finally returning to Shanghai. They embarked on their literary careers for various reasons, but most of them were simply passionate about writing. The writers are involved in a variety of occupations, including university professors, literary editors, leaders of literary institutions and professional writers. The diversity of topics covered in these novellas will lead readers to discover the different experiences and motivations of the authors. Readers will encounter a fascinating range of esthetic convictions as they analyze the authors' distinctive artistic skills and writing styles. Generally speaking, a realistic writing style dominates most of their literary works. The literary works they have elaborately created are a true reflection of drastic social changes, as well as differing perspectives towards urban life in Shanghai. Some works created by avant-garde writers have been selected in order to present a variety of styles. No matter what writing styles they adopt though, these writers have enjoyed a definite place, and exerted a positive influence, in Chinese literary circles over the past three decades.

Known as the "Paris of the Orient" around the world, Shanghai was already an international metropolis in the 1920's and 1930's. During that period, Shanghai was China's economic, cultural and literary center. A high number of famous Chinese writers lived, created and published their literary works in Shanghai, including, Lu Xun, Guo Moruo, Mao Dun and Ba Jin. Today, Shanghai has become a globalized metropolis. Writers who have pursued a literary career in the past 30 years are now faced with new challenges and opportunities. I am confident that some of them will produce other fine and influential literary works in the future. I want to make it clear that this set of pocket books does not include all representative Shanghai writers. When the time is ripe, we will introduce more representative writers to readers in the English-speaking world.

Wang Jiren
Series Editor

Contents

The Messenger's Letter

Of course, he was simply a messenger, and he didn't know anything about the letter he was delivering. However, the look in his eyes, his smile and his whole manner seemed to reveal something, even though he didn't realize it himself.

—Franz Kafka

The poet stood on the long and narrow road said: There, a needle is sewing together time with a holy water.

The sky belonged to the migrating birds. They had been circling in front of the Messenger's gloomy eyes for many centuries. Their soaring movements made the Messenger's eyeballs ache. So, in the Messenger's imagination these winter roads had long been mysterious and holy. The possibilities of endless centuries opened before the messenger as he passed along them.

The wind, frustrated and angry, swept across the sky of migrating birds with a sigh.

The Messenger's journeys were peaceful, and their memories were sleeping. Amongst the leisurely life of a messenger, my lust was awakened in vain. The Messenger communicated with a conventional world. The pleasures of life were something for the future.

The Messenger woke up together with the one called God on the same ordinary morning. As God did his fifth exercise, headstands, the Messenger's naked feet waded through the virgin spring towards the sea of dust.

We know there was one who saw this upside down scene. He could also see the letters floating like a feather from the Messenger's arms. No one would collect them all, because the street cleaner was still dreaming, and God's workout had already reached the sixth exercise, the pantomime pose.

The Messenger descended to a bountiful land. He had to pass through the outskirts of time before he could enter that city of penance and humiliation.

God was a little hard of hearing. As a primary school student he was mischievous, and had been beaten until half-crippled by the old maid who taught Chinese. The place the Messenger was heading for was called the Whispering City. For God, it did not even exist.

The people of the Whispering City lived among sweet snippets of time. On the avenue of time crowds of people, men and women, young and old, were staggering along like ants. Their fervent lips were parted in gestures of intense expectation. Their puzzled expressions seemed to be a kind of exhortation, a hint that they were in the midst of a self-indulgent fantasy.

Their unchanging history swept across their flaming and reed like brows. It peered into their inner beings at will, constantly harassing their souls. In dejected silence, their mournful eyes gazed at the messenger's sleepwalking hallucinations.

The letter was a sentimental and rustic exile.

I began to feel that the Messenger was from some fictional city in a book. He drew nearer to the gradually receding figures and the rainy scene, nearer to the bitter winter wind lashing the windows of warm houses, closer to the lazy dust falling slowly in the light. The people of the Whispering City waved their strong arms gently in the evening twilight. The messenger understood at once that this was a joining of the seasons, a quick sketch of feelings, a mass writing of erotic sentences.

The letter quoted from the old scriptures

for its own ends.

The Messenger listened over and over to the indistinct voices all around him. Terrified, his heart fell into a fast, palpitating rhythm. I held on to my feelings towards home, the naive sentiments that had been lost to me, and my irrational belief in the beauty of the street scene before me.

The letter was a stranger playing his part in some unknown journey.

Everywhere on the night streets there were sad partings from pleasant dreams. Many stories would be forgotten, never to be heard again. The letter would float away. Like a traditional song it could be adapted to suit different occasions and people would do what they wanted with it.

The letter was a remote and otherworldly revelation.

It would inevitably become a pile of scrap paper after people tired of reading it. The setting sun was already out of sight. The distinct sound of water could be heard in the darkness. If I did not find a place to stay for the night, I would no longer be a conscientious messenger.

The Messenger considered the contents of the letter: perhaps they were expressed in a melody (in music), in the warm lip marks on a just played instrument (in any kind of process), in the movement of the air after someone sighs (in sentimental reflections), in listening expectantly to discover something (in hesitating over what is rational), in the absence of human activity (in becoming one with nature), in the deep love underlying the whole of nature (in the journey towards transcendence), in ostentatious contemplation before a bloody bas-relief (in a deep skepticism of the human mind), in confused wandering and a pleasant stroll (in the examination of daily life), in desire for a new dawn (in hoping for good fortune), in the banishment of darkness (in perfection), in the violent twisting of abstract lines (in endless seeking), in air, water and seasons (in the whole of life), in rotting, infested earth and the fragrance of new life (in temptation and the resistance of temptation), in writing, in sending, in delivering, in receiving, and in reading (in the Messenger's letter).

The letter was a state of affairs.

Its readers were everywhere.

The letter was a kind of tentative self-seeking, a mischievous but worthy pride. It was a cautious alteration of the individual and an unintentional disclosure.

"The Messenger's Letter" was a popular song long ago, the anthem of an irresistible sleep. The ill-tempered writer of the song was also a messenger. One day, in an adolescent reverie of mine, he took me to a dirty corner of a quiet street. In the dream he pulled out a crumpled envelope, and held it in front of my eyes. He casually said to me:

"Kid, take it, it's a present from me to you." This was the renowned song. As he gave it to me, I started singing it in my dream. Afterwards I found out that, that night, he drank more than usual. A while later this poetic, wine-loving messenger breathed his last when he went to take in the fresh air of the summer night.

The wind scattered the clouds, and morning came. Before setting off I was still trying to shake off the after effects of a deep sleep. The murmurs of the night had disappeared with the first light of dawn. The doors along the street were about to open. Only a messenger would go calling on people at the break of day. The sad truth was out, but nobody knew about the hard night I'd spent.

The letter was merely a gasp for breath.

Day and night the star gazer lost himself in a terrifying emotional lake. The Messenger's quick steps were like two waves of fate. The Messenger followed rushing time, my keen blood pulsing continually through my exhausted body.

The letter was a hand on a disconcerting clock.

In the little known history of the Whispering City, there was a certain period that the people tried their best not to think about. Every day, the dawn light shone down on the streets. The morning brilliance rescued the cold streets from an indescribable tragedy with its brilliant splendor.

The letter was a curtain falling over the Whispering City.

The avenue was overshadowed by

another one. The days there passed quietly in a colorless hush. The one shaking his legs in the cold wind on the street corner was not some adolescent young hooligan. He was there to salute me. He told me that he was once a navigator.

"The Messenger was born with a nightwalker's face. Look at me. I'm the last relic of the great age of snow."

I could not make out what he was muttering. "I stand at the side of the street, like a sailor standing on deck."

The letter was a rising of the anchor at the start of an uncertain, lonely voyage.

At that time, people were crazy about voyages. They needed salt covered cuts to add fire and purpose to their trivial dreams.

The letter was a cathartic release of emotional suffering.

"In my whole life, you are the first person

to come and salute me," the Messenger said.

"Moreover, I am the last person to salute you, because I am the only one at my post in the Whispering City," replied the greeter.

The letter was like the long calm between two riotous festivals, a pause for breath between shouts, sanity faking dizziness.

Nobody knew where the greeter came from. In the Whispering City the greeter had to be a person of wide ranging knowledge, but at the same time a quiet and retiring sage. The romantic experiences of the navigator's seafaring career gave him an encyclopedic knowledge of the world, and an equally immense love of solitude. He was well-qualified for the mission. He described for me the memories he had of his first night: my gut reaction was that he was lying to me.

The letter was a dull, forever repeating pattern.

"From a certain way of looking at things, we are the same, the messenger walking over the land, the navigator crossing the sea. I'd even say a messenger is also a guard."

"So, we can salute each other."

"No, we can pull tongues at each other!" laughed the greeter.

The letter was a magic wand waved by hypocrites.

"The Whispering City has plenty of fantastic places to visit at night." He could see I wasn't interested, and quickly blurted out: "The baths, the smoking rooms, the taverns, the money houses, the …"

"Crowded, chaotic places you mean."

"No, no, hardly anyone goes to these kinds of places anymore."

The messenger thought to himself: the letter is like a summer vine. He thought again: No, maybe it is more a musical interlude in some wonderful circus show.

"Bustling, crowded places just make people feel more lonely." How could the citizens of The Whispering City, dignified and graceful as they were, submit themselves to such nauseating pushing and shoving?

The letter was like the faint whispers of a recluse.

"Even so, I would like to take a stroll around these places." I came to the Whispering City to deliver a letter.

"The letter can't be for me, I haven't received any letters for years. When I was at sea I used to write letters to myself. After every voyage I would read these letters from the sea. Since I stopped going to sea, I haven't had the pleasure of reading like that."

"It makes me sad to see you so desolate, but this letter was clearly not sent from the sea, it has merely been sent by way of the sea from another land. I don't think it's yours."

"Yes, this letter is definitely meant for

someone other than me."

Most people in the Whispering City were not like the greeter. They were born with hard, proud faces. Old or young, man or woman, they all walked along the dirty streets in a fearless and haughty manner.

When the Messenger hurried to the notice board first thing in the morning, he arrived just in time to witness a mass brawl. The ring leader whispered something to the people around him, leaving them baying for a fight. But after he finished speaking, he disappeared. Some of the crowd threw themselves whole heartedly into the fight; others surrounded the scene to see what would happen. Enthusiasm was written all over their faces, but due to their natural reserve, they stood feigning indifference and watched.

The letter was a gesture of hatred, a malevolent chant unleashing violence and loneliness.

And that's what I found. I heard from those around that public brawls had become a popular distraction in the Whispering City.

The letter was like the dream of a gully to become a bottomless abyss.

Let the beautiful weather shine down, and save the letter from becoming empty nonsense.

Just like every great race throughout history, the citizens of the Whispering City had a holy place that was the focus of their pride. Near the cattle pens of a farm on the outskirts of the City were the ruins of an ancient courtyard. On an afternoon that will one day be forgotten, the Messenger arrived there.

The monk's market. I first heard this strange name from the wrinkled guard.

The valley was green and the earth fragrant, everything bathed in brilliant sunlight. In the intense brightness the threatening, solid shapes of the mountains were visible, but the whole earth was filled with fresh exuberance. If someone was looking from a distance, I would have looked like a simple pilgrim, stumbling along the rough track on the outskirts of the town.

There was indeed someone who saw the messenger. His happy face appeared at his window. As the Messenger drew closer, the monk's market revealed its own mournful routine. I was ready to believe that the journey was about to end right there. I was under orders to bring the message to its final destination. When the receiver appeared next to the corral, the whole matter would reach a conclusion.

The letter was a secret meeting between desperate lovers.

This one that the Messenger imagined to be the receiver was a cultured monk. He was popular in the monk's market at the time. There was no way of tracing his ancestry, but he was full of extravagant stories. To his listeners it seemed that he would need the rest of his life to finish his memoir: *My Life in the Royal Palace.*

In the long and kaleidoscopic past of the Whispering City and its people, the goings on at the palace had always been the main talking point for all classes. There were hundreds of ragged, starving performers. For their whole lives they never got bored of talking about palace secrets in their pure, naive way. They would sit under one another's eaves talking no matter what the weather. They reveled in any opportunity to talk about the romance of the past, recalling the affairs played out in such and such a dynasty, or this or that palace garden. The

Messenger saw that, apart from their idle speculation about the great happenings in the palace, their lives were empty and unremarkable.

The letter was the beautiful martyrdom of a coward.

Compared with those dispossessed and restless spirits, the author of *My Life in the Royal Palace* clearly came from a more "noble" background. His pride in his noble blood and the wide learning he had picked up with absent-minded ease led him to take liberties with reality. In his fanciful imagination, he lived in some imaginary ancient palace. The Messenger was skeptical.

By the end of the year, the Messenger still wouldn't know the name of the cultured monk, whose tears began flowing before he had even written anything. In the midst of his poetic weeping he began to describe the sad history of the palace.

The letter was a terrifying leap over the abyss.

I came to the window of the weary looking writer. I thought he would say a few words to me before he continued working on one of his tedious paragraphs. The Messenger had not come to console him.

The letter was a streak of rouge passing itself off as the rose-pink light of dawn.

The window was left open in a welcoming manner, and the sound of pages turning could be heard inside. The sound made the Messenger feel warm and drew him in.

"It's incredible that you are actually here disturbing me." He spoke to me like a preacher. In a very relaxed manner he leaned against the window frame, and stretched out his neck towards me.

"I'm writing about friendship, love and death. I'm writing in an ambiguous style, trying to make each sentence as preposterous as I can. Do you think it's impossible?"

I watched him take his thumb out of his mouth, and then put in his forefinger and middle finger one after the other.

"Will it take a long time to write the book?"

"Yes, because I still have to write about the funerals of the dead, and the recollections of the living. Tell me, in this world are there any more torturous ways to waste time than funerals or sentimental reminiscences? I think not … apart from me repeating it all on the page that is."

"People say that you lived in the palace for many years."

"It's difficult to say. I'll only be able to answer that question when I finish writing the book. People should not come to such hasty conclusions. We should at least look at what is written on the page."

"So where do you get the ideas for your

book?"

He smiled serenely: "From writing!"

The letter was an announcement of God's vacation.

"May I look at a few paragraphs of your book?"

"Which part do you want to read? Women with silk shawls? Wine and poker games? Or maybe an autumn outing that ends in disappointment."

"Anything is fine. It's up to you."

"If it's up to me, it's better if you don't read anything. You should really start reading from the crucial story of the mountain, but I haven't written that chapter yet."

The letter was a gentle, illusory silence.

"Aren't you going to ask where I'm from?" The Messenger put his arms on the window frame. "I just might be from the palace you are writing about in your book. It's not totally impossible."

It seemed to the Messenger that this gifted writer was afraid of something regarding his book.

"It's my palace!" The monk shouted out righteously.

That was how the monk writer died. He probably died from an angry rage. I don't know if there are any other instances of this kind of death in the history of the Whispering City. As the Messenger is ready to talk about another monk now, the best thing to do is let him die.

May his book rest in peace.

The monk was actually a nun. She could lie on a haystack in the winter sun for days without getting up. People near and far called her by a beautiful name: Gentle Lily. But in actual fact this woman was a murderer and a thief. She often opened the skulls of living victims, and devoured their scrambled thoughts.

She had innumerable lovers, who came to the Whispering City and the surrounding mountains like fugitives. Every spring, they scampered back to her like wild rabbits to await her loving attentions.

"I can keep myself pure. My thoughts are sublime, because I'm higher than the things of this world. My occasional vices are the result of my sexual desires. I've had enough of rushing about like an animal. There's an old monkish saying: Stillness is the most profound kind of movement."

The letter was like an impotent member recalling its former conquests.

At four o'clock in the afternoon, Gentle Lily feebly raised her pure white arms in the fading breeze. She used her fingers to nonchalantly smooth her oily black hair back behind her head. At that moment, there was only the eternal sun outside the window and the sound of her sighing at the memory of her first kiss.

She spoke like all women who have been unlucky in love, but she couldn't continue.

The letter was the ensign of first love.

He was a man on the run. In winter time, with swirling patterns of ice spread over the windows, he would sit there doing nothing, or burn papers covered with random scrawl. When he was young he witnessed several infamous upheavals. Gradually he lost heart and passion, and began to grumble about everything. When he fiercely swore that he would never return on that sunny autumn day, the people of the City regarded him as another victim of troubled times. Later, smothered with unending loving care day after day, he snapped, entering a frenzy of self-mutilation in the autumn streets that he could not pull back from. His lips trembled from mental confusion. When Lily, still half asleep, rushed onto the street, the features of his face were already a twisted, bloody mess. Finally, he took his idiotic, hideous face and left the Whispering City.

The letter was like a vague impotence of time.

Some long-distance travelers came across him on the post road. He told everyone he met his plans to burn himself, because he could see the only house. "Beside the door I opened there was another door. Through the door I opened I could see two more open doors. Now it was my turn to open the closed door."

"I want to open that door," the nun said.

It was the people of the City that buried him. As everybody knows, from ancient times in the Whispering City there were only a small amount of saints who were granted a state funeral when they died. They were all scruffy jugglers and artists that performed tricks on the streets.

When the nun's lover still had a boyish face, he was as delicate as an imperial silk scroll. He was terrified by any kind of commotion in the streets. In a state of great apprehension he was told that, as a chosen one, he had to make public the details of his trances in the middle of the monk's square for the next hundred to a hundred and fifty years.

"Oh the kind, caring people of the Whispering City ..." he croaked, shaking all over.

The letter was a pile of firewood desperate for someone to light the match.

Surrounding him were a group of giant dwarves. As they were desperate to be giants, there was an office in the City specifically for settling family disputes that graciously allowed them to be small giants. "The only thing that goes unpunished in this city is

talking nonsense. Brainless idiots! It really
is a disgrace to the City."

The letter was a eulogy to dead feelings.

As the nun thought about her past, she
looked sad and elegant. "Let's go to the saw
mill," she said.

The Messenger saw the greeter smoking
cigarettes in a forest of camphor trees near
the saw mill. "I take some time out to come
here every week." Together we wandered
around the fragrant forest, waiting to enter
the crowded mill.

In the Whispering City the word
"saw mill" also had the same meaning as
"temple." People came here for the sacred
wood, which could console their wasted
hearts. This sweet-smelling wood had just
been cut from a log filled with tree rings.
But it was given away for free. The people
affectionately referred to this wood as the
spring of dignity.

The letter was a constant inner monologue.

"Adulterer!" The nun let out a sensual moan that floated through the leaves of the camphor trees and filled the air around the greeter.

This forest scene would undoubtedly have made the most erotic chapter of the Messenger's journey. However, it would have to be omitted by the usually diligent Messenger. The Messenger would only touch upon the sweet anticipation, the light touch of skin, or the post-coital bliss.

The letter was an absurd resurrection.

Under the midday sun, in an occasional spell of winter warmth that I can hardly describe convincingly, the undisputed author of *My Life in the Royal Palace* sucked on a piece of wood. He had a proud expression on his face and his toes were turned outwards. With long, solemn steps he steadily drew closer.

"The earth is soft," he said. His red face revealed his excitement about returning to the world.

"There!" I guessed he was pointing to Hell.

"There!" He repeated, trying to build a dramatic effect.

"There!" He continued, chanting the refrain. "God dam it, I never even saw one of the City people there."

Where was he actually pointing to? Where? Where? Apart from bombarding the resurrected one with repetitive questions, the Messenger had no other short cuts to the truth. Endless wandering would not necessarily allow the Messenger to perceive the way back from the world beyond.

"I really have rotten god dam luck. There was a festival every day there, no way of getting away from it even for a second. Birth-

days, remembrance days, name days, anni-
versaries, annual celebrations, centennial
celebrations, millennial celebrations, ten
thousand year celebrations, days to com-
memorate resting, 365 days, no quiet moments. Jesus, I've come back for a vacation!
I want to have a proper rest like real people
do!" The ghost took great gulps of fresh air.
I guess that was down to the stuffiness of
the saw mill.

While he was talking, his plump cheeks
grew redder. Pretty soon, he would be fit for
the role of a lover.

The Messenger turned his head. The
nun's stare was fixed on the sparkling light
flashing between the trees. "You are a
gleaming skeleton," she said angrily.

The letter was like a well-kept secret
shared by a married couple.

The distance between the Messenger and
the letter was like the distance between the

outer world and an inner flash of thought. It was an all-pervading, bewildering space. The Messenger was the letter's unruly vassal.

The letter was a random, non-existent indulgence of the Messenger.

"I am your one true love. To tell you the truth, I found out there that you told some passers-by about your passion on the haystack, and that deep down the one you really care for isn't me. You're so cruel!" After he said this, the spirit gulped. "Surely you haven't completely forgotten about all our sweet kisses and hugs in the study."

"What study? The study in that far-flung palace?" the nun replied sarcastically.

"God damn it. Yes!"

When the greeter saw the two lovers like this, though inseparable after their hard experiences through life and death, he couldn't help feeling dejected.

"We lived a boring life among moral strictures that blotted out the real world, creating the incomparably long history of the Whispering City in our mediocre but unusual way. In our remote past that dazzles us with its brilliance, the Whispering City's pure and simple sages destroyed the few rose gardens still existing in people's imaginations first. Then they carefully picked a crisp autumn day, and with their faces turned to the sky looked up at the surrounding mountains, longing for some pure and rational holy place in the far depths of the universe to save their hearts. Even though we cannot hear its spiritual excitement or faint whispers, perhaps we can peek at several worldly parts of the holy place. From ancient times, the oracle keepers of the Whispering City, tortured by simple wisdom, have had these kinds of ridiculous desires their whole lives."

The letter was an endless anthem of love.

The Messenger rested on a sagging wall that was gradually sinking into the mud. The cool evening sunshine was silently saying its daily farewell to the couch grass standing uncut on the streets. The evening breeze blew gently. I spotted the greeter clasping his hands together, eyeing up the mules and horses hurrying along the street.

"Mrs. Zhang Wang."

"Mrs. Li Zhao."

"Mrs. Zhou."

"Mrs. Qin."

He expressed his nighttime passions in a warbling voice.

"Who are you calling to?"

"Those beasts." His reply came out lifeless as a cold stone. With these words, trampling on the silent broken stones, he hopped away.

In a corner of the Whispering City, it was just about that time of the evening for flying kites.

"Kites." The people of the City called them paper birds, cloth butterflies, or bamboo eagles. They were the only way that the people wandering over the Earth could touch the unreachable heavens. Besides, it was a way of transcending earthly disputes, an exquisite delusion.

Flying kites was the evening entertainment of the people, a part of their routine just as much as brushing their teeth at night.

A five tone idyll served as the epic musical accompaniment to the racing figures, scampering after the wind with kites in their hands in the lingering dusk. This monotonous humming was like a kind soul occasionally tripping over words as they read them swiftly and quietly. The busy fields were filled with an unusual harmony.

The letter was a slowly ensuing cruelty on the field of faith.

That group of haggard monks came in crowds over the horizon before me. They walked along with helpless and mournful expressions, drawn in by fate in spite of themselves, just like the Messenger was. They were like sons of heaven standing in the haze of the distant, radiant sunset, full of admiration for the splendors of nature surrounding them. With their cotton thread in hand, they guided along their multi-colored toys, playing their cult game.

The letter was a puzzling and extravagant interview with a rebellious heretic.

Gentle Lily's dress flowed in the wind. Walking with deliberate steps she led a nimble butterfly through the shifting wind, executing magical shifts in the air that were like the whispered promises of a lover. There was no trace of any goblins in the peaceful fields. You could see the rustic habits of the people everywhere you looked. Womanly superstitions had long been buried deep in the past, along with freak events. Small groups of travelers played the same tired old games in the pure and flawless twilight.

The nun walked across my path, opening her hand towards me: "We are six-fingered people."

The Messenger saw that they were indeed experts at brushing the night breeze. In my future memories, the meaning of life in the City would become unclear. Their far-removed symbols and chosen metaphors would show themselves for a split-second, sketching their hidden defects on the flawless magic mirror of space and time.

The letter was a shallow affection for ruins.

The weather was sunny and cloudless. An impulse led me to follow the greeter along the dark street to the Monk's Market, which smelled strongly of medicine.

"You! Are you latecomers?" A young monk said, blocking our path.

"No, I'm here to see someone." I said, stepping forward.

"You won't find anyone now. Everyone is at the funeral for the legendary characters. They won't be back for several hours."

"Can I just go take a look? Maybe I will come across the person I'm looking for."

"Alright then …." He said reluctantly. "I never realized that the living could be so persistent. Look along the next few blocks. Maybe you can catch up with them."

"Which way did they go?"

"Every way."

The messenger had come from a far off, real place. He had set out at a moment that was difficult to describe in detail. Now, those first impressions have come back to me from some far away place. All the journeys made before mine, and my own journey, have trickled together to become one.

My narration probably seems to have quietly separated from my experiences in the Whispering City, leaving the reader Adam-like, begging to take a bite of the forbidden fruit.

The letter is the stripping bare of something, description by description.

The evening breeze blew towards those idolaters, who were intoxicated by legend. All around me they wandered around in a daze. With the wretchedness of beggars, they invited sympathy. With the indifference of executioners, they became the bell ringers of morning death.

The letter is a futile self-introduction to a partner at a masked ball.

The six-fingered people conducted their military march, dragging along their weapons as they went, solemnly posing or firing recklessly into the air in order to enjoy themselves. They shot the deep red paper ornaments blowing in the wind near the window lattices. Then they suddenly turned around. Moaning and groaning, they chased after a group of women, stomping along in their small and wide heels, and then shooting their lace petticoats. They liked the smell of cotton and silk. "Smell! Smell! Smell!" The six-fingered people were running around everywhere like uncontrollable rams. They dashed around obscurely like lust filled shadows.

The greeter suddenly stood spellbound on the street corner and expressed his admiration. "Such delightful revels. Such fatherly indulgence. The dead mythical characters are lucky. Now they know that even at a funeral the people of the City can flirt with each other, they will really repent the fact that they cannot be reborn in this world."

"It's very exciting. What a wonderful scene." Even a person as ignorant as me could be moved by this, and could see that the monk's market really was no ordinary place.

The six-fingered people were like skittish revelers taking delight in a festival. Like strict jailors they pushed themselves to live through an endless succession of lazy springs, drowsy summers, surreal autumns, and winters passed in death like hibernations. With their motionless grandeur they imitated a martyr's beautiful pose. With their cruel jokes they summoned up their simple feelings. Their appearance before the funeral started was a combination of manic make-up and horrible masks.

"Are they afraid of ceremonies? Are they allowed on these streets?"

"The six-fingered make sacrifices, but they aren't the sacrifices of a warrior, they are the sacrifices of a jailor. They share the prison with their prisoners, but they don't share responsibility for any crimes." The greeter defended the six-fingered people, wandering around panic stricken before the funeral. "Their tragedy is the jailor's tragedy, giving up their freedom voluntarily."

The letter was intoxicated by the late autumn gloom's incessant soliloquy.

"Don't tell me that rattle of rifles also counts as a sacrifice?" The people of the City really did make a big deal out of nothing.

"What else could be more enchanting to them than the slow raising of a flag to half mast?"

"How can they explain away the indulgent passions of their hearts as a sacrifice?"

"Perhaps the stress and bitterness of their pain is as eternally fearful as a funeral song?

"Grief should be bitter and undisturbed, not the furor that the six-fingered people make of it." When the Messenger saw that the nun and her late lover were also mingling with the crowd, he could not help having serious doubts about the integrity of the funeral.

"They are searching for the qi that flows inside them, and then they will write funeral couplets along the walls."

"The way I see it, these occasions should be properly planned in good time. This is just like a sideshow."

The six-fingered people used their immense strength to write a whirlwind of characters. Although the handwriting was rushed and crude, in every character lay hidden an abstract beauty. The monks wrote enthusiastically, losing all sense of their surroundings. They worked themselves into such a frenzy that they ended up huddled together, each using all 12 fingers to write parallel lines of wild script.

The Messenger seemed to have bad eyesight. Even though the words were strung out in front of him, he still could not grasp their meaning. The funeral couplets were full of everyday, vulgar flatteries. They seemed to be a kind of remedy to counteract the pain of death.

"God dam! God dam!" the monks said over and over.

I stood off to one side, as if I was standing next to a temple that did not exist in human imagination. The Messenger had a hazy emotional connection with these strangers.

The letter is examining an unknown state of affairs from an unknown point of view.

In the exuberance surrounding me I gradually realized: The Messenger was not searching for a definite receiver for the letter.

Only in the seeking would the Messenger gradually understand who it was. Could I possibly find him among the six-fingered monks of the Whispering City? If the answer was no, would I be able to create a new character to replace the ignorant masses of this City that bewildered the Messenger?

Supposing the answer was still no. Would the Messenger still have the courage to continue with his mission through such uncertainty?

If wandering in itself was the purpose, I would only be able to regard the walking as an aimless stroll.

Although the monks were malnourished, all in all they were full of learning. Thanks to the din they made charging in like wild horses, shouting and uproar replaced the respectful silence of a funeral.

The Messenger and the greeter were squeezed between the gun wielding six-fingered people. The nun and her controversial number one lover were sucking and slurping each other under a cane shaded window.

"You really are unmoved by an intimate act like that," the greeter said, and put his delicate hand on my shoulder. I did not need the help of any kind of divine light to understand what he meant. I clearly saw six fingers extending from his pale hand. Next to his stubby little finger protruded a sixth finger, demonically thrusting itself into the world.

"Disciples of violence, just like the book of physiognomy says." When he saw me staring in fascination at the mark of his clan, he began an aggressive explanation of the freakish form of himself and those like him. As the greeter's body inched towards me, it became obvious that he wanted to snuggle up to me. "Don't get too close to the female,go for the masculine." I don't know if this line is in the book of physiognomy.

The greeter's voice was thick and trembling. Through his uncontrollable groans, the Messenger heard about the love affairs of an insincere man bothered by vanity and hurt.

The six-fingered people were weak and sentimental. Their eyes were unusually long and narrow, and their noses unsightly and wide. This made it difficult for them to show many emotions, even if inside they were full of tenderness. Most of them were from rich and powerful families. From childhood they forged an indissoluble bond with "the four treasures" of the scholar. Their childhood practical jokes were usually recorded in 3 to 7 word annotated verses. Their free and easy childhoods were written in neat, regulated verse, containing their preposterous and degenerate ideas. The short and tasteful affairs of their adulthood were expressed in crashing, masterful songs. Their unspoken, immortal wishes were found in their collections of elegant parallel prose. Their dying wish was to have a tombstone beside the road inscribed with imposing calligraphy.

The golden age of the six-fingered people made a deep imprint in the ancient books. After the repeated reading and scrutiny of generation after generation, the mystery of those events had lost all poetic grandeur and they were now forgotten. Living in hovels, they had to use the feeble winter wind to moisten their chapped skin.

Looking back, the thing that touched me was that their roots did after all lay in a group that had passed on knowledge for generations. At least they were able to shake themselves from their trance; at least they were able to shout out their centuries old desires in the long drawn out voice of a comedy clown.

The letter was a suicide performed in the bravado of drunkenness.

"You're tickling me, you lout!" I said. I couldn't bear that kind of sickening touch. Being in the lifeless funeral procession was the same as shouting blasphemies against the creator.

The six-fingered people all gave me black looks to shut me up. "Don't be like that. I'm a Messenger!" I couldn't help trembling.

Their stare had a monk's delicacy that was made up of a painful infatuation and an indignant recollection, full of the indistinct sadness of the setting sun. They were like an unfathomable part of history.

Silent musing had sent grief out of the world, into the realms of freedom and happiness. The greeter skipped through the barren soil of his love story.

As the funeral procession passed by, the streets were empty. A light wind blew between the buildings, sending dead twigs and leaves swirling around the deserted streets. It carried away the waste paper and fruit skins dropped by passers by at the foot of the wall and the crossroads, performed a few dancers' twirls, and then cast them away like old shoes. It affectionately played with the greasy things in the gutters and doorways. Then, piercing the streets or cloisters close by, it suddenly disappeared again without a trace.

The way of thinking of the six-fingered people was to sneak and stoop around with a humble attitude. Their illicit meetings under the eaves, between the black tiles and white walls, did not bother the ants marching their route. They grasped at a putrid and unfathomable slyness on edge of an extraordinarily deep vat of rice wine.

They passed off the silence and emptiness of a dried up well for a cry to the heavens. Among the gnarly and twisted roots of the trees they set themselves up as heroes on a mission to punish wrongdoers. They looked out on the great open land from feeble dike tops.

"All in all, we are like sand and water mixed together." The greeter seemed to be describing some ethical creed of the six-fingered people.

The thing they valued above all else was bravery. The thing they despised the most was a muddy blade. They came from the country of the fish people in the sea. They were still weeping for their ancestors on the island.

"Who are you saving yourself for?"

"I am a flatfooted, portly, rotten-toothed Messenger." I didn't care whether or not the island of the six-fingered people had disappeared in a deluge beneath the sea. I shoved him away.

The letter was the rocking journey of the ark.

The object of the Messenger's passionate sighs was a follower of the beauty of words. She had to have courage to enter my uncontrollable and wild imagination as if she knew she was making a certain mistake. She had to regard an unfinished journey as a road of escape. She stood there trying to make sense of her confused thoughts. At that moment the nun approaching me had rivers of motherly tears on her face and a wanderer's nostalgia. She approached seductively.

"I'm always fond of travelers rushing along the road. They attract me with their hurried, cautious looks."

"I like those I meet too. Their unbreakable spirit is something to behold."

The Messenger and the nun carried on their pointless and cagey talk amidst the rumbling of the funeral salute.

The funeral of these homeless immortals had its own sacred trivialities. Fires and anthems burst out at the same time. In the dizzying light around me, my awareness moved from a numb desperation towards a cathartic emptiness. Their red skin and broad, pulsing veins were driving them into an incessant uproar like wild studs. In an instant, time and direction were split apart by the welling up of a flood of desire. Southerly grief lingered on without end in the sky above the flat earth, as the six-fingered people began extending their distorted fingers towards the legendary characters.

After some other matters that we will omit here, at the home of the phoenix, we gropingly offered our hands to each other.

The whole poetic scene was recorded for
future generations by meticulous scribes
on rice paper thin as butterfly wings. In a
brief moment of calm before the flood, the
image of love making flashed before me.
Impulsive sinking evolved into a sinking
impulsiveness from West to East. The idea
had been cherished in the deepest recesses
of their history. Hereditary serving-girls
hung their angry wishes on the branches
of ancient trees that reached into the skies.
This speculative canopy was only for bug-
eyed spiders crawling on their webs. The
middle of the trees was full of explorers
hacking their way through, their fragile
bones creaking as they moved against each
other. Their native homes required them to
return to their places of ancestry when they
got old, and their dialects gagged them. In
the dots and dashes of an ancient almanac,
the world weary travelers discovered the

predestined, auspicious day to go home.

Ah. What a blessing.

The length of the funeral made it impossible for the Messenger to maintain his composure. The way I see it, the Whispering City is able use its vices to subdue all messengers.

"I'm tired," the Messenger almost begged the nun.

"Nobody is looking to take a breather. The most joyous part of the funeral is about to start. You should hold on a while."

"What kind of joy can there be at a funeral?"

"You can dance with a dead one you love. This is a rare opportunity. You better think carefully about who you want to dance with, so you don't end up with the wrong one when the time comes."

The Messenger didn't know who was among the dead, but anyway I had no interest in dancing. "I'll just stand and watch; maybe I will see the one I'm looking for."

"That's impossible. There's no one apart from doctors and soldiers among the dead ones. They never do anything except treat other people's sicknesses or suffer illness themselves."

Through the nun's words I saw that the Messenger would not be able to escape her prejudice and pride. To the accompaniment of a refined piece of music, the people started to dance with their partners.

The letter is a warning: the body needs rest.

Every step forward the Messenger took had some newly revealed truth to tell me. Life already existed in a way that I knew nothing about. The Messenger pondered: the known and the unknown both exist in this world. Beyond my experience and knowledge, there was a wider, mysterious world. The things it contains are certainly not waiting anxiously for me to reach them; they are simply waiting for their own destiny beyond my uneasy consciousness. It is impossible for me to brush past them all at the same time.

The letter is an endlessly repeated empty slogan.

I could not remember any impressive dance steps. The Messenger's feet stumbled woodenly forward, so that my dancing looked like the reflection of my obscure feelings. After the music stopped, the swirling traces of my footprints became a cold maze of confusion.

In this entertaining interlude full of music and dancing, the nun's hate filled assertion of the Messenger's faults had melted away in my deep thoughts. The nun's first love called her in a loud, clear voice, and leaving me standing there she ran to him. With that posture against the background of the pale street scene, she seemed to be saying: I am a lady who lives life the way I want, not one of those attractive women who are impossible to willingly entice. The silhouette of them walking off together seemed like a doomsday ensemble.

The letter is a forever out of date document.

"He's there," said the nun, the moment she turned the corner.

Who did she mean? And where was "there"? Nobody knew, including the Messenger. I gave up attempting to find out from those ahead of me.

This scene of whispers and purity left my eyes full of tears. People walking through light and darkness, day and night! Your esthetic is in all that the Messenger sees and hears.

I had missed my only chance. I felt that

from then on there would be no one to tell the Messenger where somebody was.

The letter was simply a proposition.

I wondered if, at that earthly ceremony, the legendary characters would perform a dramatic ascension towards heaven in the extraordinary way that people imagine. The Whispering City, diligently built by the six-fingered people and innumerable nuns and monks (perhaps also including cripples and hunchbacks), really was a divine song from heaven played on the celestial earth.

The letter was the conclusion of a legend.

When we open a letter, we are opening up a story from the past along with others. The writer of the letter is one role in the story, the reader is another role. The Messenger is the plot, the suspense, the outsider, the prodigal son driven by pride, and the stranger that everyone is familiar with.

This was the time that people call the night. At dusk the day disappeared behind the night, to await its next appearance. A person was approaching me out of the darkness.

"Who are you?" he asked me, seeming like a practitioner of daoist voodoo in the dark.

"No one has ever asked me that before."

"Why not?" he shot back, his deep voice coming closer, but his figure still hidden.

"It's obvious." I quickly recalled my whole life. To my surprise I found that, in this dreamlike interrogation, the Messenger, who tended towards worshipping himself, was at the same time not himself. I was actually any other person but myself.

"Impossible. There's only one man in the world that's obvious, and that's me."

"And who are you?" I still could not see where the voice was coming from.

"A legendary dead man."

"What did you do when you were alive?" I wanted to find out what this invisible man looked like.

"I was a dead man when I was alive. I was created by the people of the City and written into a legend as a dead man." His words chilled me to the bone.

"By the sound of your voice, you're a friendly person. Can you let me have a look at your face?" I discovered that I was timid as well as stupid.

"The six-fingered people didn't get round to my face."

"Ah, what neglect. With those six-fingered hands of theirs they should definitely have created a good face for you. It's a shame. Then I'll tell you who I am." The Messenger checked that no one else was around, then boldly continued. "I'm writing a book. Do you know what a book is? A book is made when people use a pen or lots of pens to write and write on very thick paper. But you already know that. *My Life in the Royal Palace* is such a book. Writing it is a task that makes a man feel dizzy and frozen. After I finish writing it, I will still have to cut out many parts that could easily lead to misunderstandings due to their byzantine descriptions.

"For example, I gave a blow-by-blow account of how the secretary of state would linger to smell the fragrant flowers under the window of the concubines' quarters before going to give his morning report to the emperor. And how he would nonchalantly walk out of the emperor's back garden when some of the concubines got up to take a piss. You can easily tell that this paragraph is full of loopholes. Firstly, the reader will find it very difficult to work out which dynasty this courtly scene belongs to; secondly, when all is said and done, if the writer has never been a secretary of state, he couldn't have stood on that path, staring at the morning beauty of the concubines peeking out from behind the archway; and finally, when would a secretary of state ever be in such a carefree and leisurely mood first thing in the morning? These words are contrary to my original intentions, and should be crossed out."

How could the Messenger talk so confidently about a work that was entirely in his own head? Did I intend to enter into some kind of collective delusion? It seemed that his willpower was unable to suppress his habit of telling lies.

"However, when someone wants to write a book there is always a reason for it. Based on my admiration for divinities, the cassock, the rush-leaf fan, and loafing about, I devoted a lot of time to writing the chapter 'The Crickets' Outing.' I didn't discuss the different categories of crickets or their particular features in my book, because that would only have resulted in criticism from the experts and headaches for the layman. Of course, veracity would undoubtedly have been praised by my descendants, but that was after all something too remote to think about at the time. What I wanted to talk about was the crickets, a hermit, a freeloader, a humble philosopher, a womanish creep, a fake woman, and a story about war."

The letter was a straight forward invasion.

"You know, if a man can't find a job working for the government, he will occupy himself with writing. For good or bad, this is something that has been part of the history of the Whispering City. My book *My Life in the Royal Palace* cannot avoid this vulgarity. At the beginning of the chapter in question, we read about a very wide road, and sunny weather coupled with glorious ideals. If I had not added the cat fights later in the narrative the story would definitely have been so clean that it would have left the purest virgins feeling ashamed. The first one to enter the story is a handsome loafer. He walks along charismatically through the solitude, before taking a rest under a tree. He falls down on the ground, obviously starving hungry. The next to appear is an experienced and prudent scholar, proficient in sign language and ventriloquism, as well as jealousy and manipulation, and other ways of dealing with people. At that time, he has not yet learned sword craft, kung fu or the use of dirty bath water to drown a child. Nevertheless, anybody can see from his pimple ridden face that he has picked up plenty of bad habits. He bends down next to the young loafer. Those who can write stories like this are clever writers. Later they can write about murder, homosexuality, friendships between men, or reconciliation between father and son. They can write about whatever they experience. They can spend a lot of time and effort writing nonsense. This is called free writing. To stop the reader losing interest due to the consecutive appearance of two male characters but no female one, and because later in the book there are no women worth writing about, the best thing is to write about creatures. The cricket, that can hop, jump, hum and call out can serve as a bright point. If I want to go to the trouble, I can write about its sister. It is also a symbol. However, the author may have a hard time explaining it in his style of writing. It serves no other purpose than to provide a dramatic climax. Next, the loafer appears, with the reddening sun as a background. Since the light is bad and my eyesight is poor, the loafer glitters all over and his outline is indistinct. Normally it is best if this kind of person hides in the background. But others say that literature should not object to crafty tricks. Nowadays it is popular to throw a mysterious character into the mix, and to build up his mysteriousness, among other techniques. However there is one who, in total contrast, does not appear on the scene for a while: the womanish creep. He is now in a far away school, measuring a band of stars using a technique that looks highly mysterious to a stranger, as if he is preparing to make them into a pleated dress. Last is the passion filled fake woman. His stocky build, and bits of stubble, and the fact that he rarely uses his worn out toothbrush, leads people to wonder whether it is B.O. or smelly feet that he suffers from.

"Firstly, they have a good look at each other under the tree, then play a game of dream interpretation. Just at this juncture, the loafer hears the chirping of the crickets ...

"Everything after that is told from the cricket's perspective. Does it make you feel bored?"

"Yes," the dead man's voice replied in the darkness.

Lucky for me he answered that way, because I would have had no idea how to continue. But hadn't the real author of *My Life in the Royal Palace* also been unable to complete the book? It seemed that this book was very difficult to finish. As we talked, the first faint light of dawn appeared in the sky. The funeral that had been so painstakingly arranged for the illustrious legendary characters was being drawn to a close among the loud wails of the nuns, in an effort to avoid a pompous spectacle, and the whole thing descending into something vulgar and messy.

The nuns nervously huddled together, humming in chorus a rather touching elegy. The Messenger could faintly hear broken snippets of the lyrics. "Majestic," "Infinite," and "Perfection" appeared again and again, so it sounded very authentic. After an unclear and drawn out "Love" there were a series of deep sighs. Those sighs were everywhere, blending together into a sustained sound of deep grieving that would usually be expressed with an "Ah!"

In an apparent effort to make the voice of the human world loud enough to reach up to heaven, the elegy ended with a deafening cheer amidst a burst of applause.

The monks and nuns dispersed, but you'd be wrong if you think that the funeral ended there. They were just catching their breath near the walls and trees, readying themselves to begin the grand procession.

It seemed to the Messenger that the

procession needed a great poet to join its
numbers if it was to be something unique
and memorable. But judging by the look of
the six-fingered people, they were probably
not interested in that kind of gaudy touch.
Funerals in the Whispering City made the
six-fingered people introverted and guilty.
Their faces were covered with faint streaks,
like engravings expressing grief.

The Messenger's travels in the City
had not allowed me to form even a rough
impression of what it contained. This
territory leading to the infinite future
seemed to be sealed off, but the halo of
some holy spirit also seemed to be hovering
in the sky above. This made it a profound
metaphor for the search for meaning. The
spirit acted in this two-dimensional way.
These broad delusions, which still had not
been woven into an ordered story, started
losing their tenuous connections.

The Messenger smiled at the people wandering past. As I was feeling happy I needed a healthy expression. The six-fingered people wailed and thronged together near the simple homes of their village. In the boundless sea of people the Messenger found it difficult to make out the shadows of those around the greeter. I think they were all overjoyed by the grandness of the public occasion. The City's people seemed to have a natural gift that ensured these transient gatherings combined an air of commemoration with a raucous atmosphere.

The letter was a handbook or rough outline of friendship.

Horn blowers and flutists passed by, followed by women and children, folk artists and street performers, authors who wanted to write important books, melancholy years and benevolent spirits, as well as gloomy talent and childish reveries. Behind there only remained the uncommunicative dead and myself, facing the Messenger's letter alone. A letter had to have a receiver. Perhaps this letter had been written for the Messenger. What I mean is that it was written for me. Supposing that was the case, what would urge the Messenger to deliver a letter to himself? Through delivering a letter to himself, would the Messenger separate from himself, and through random seeking, and the letter, would he return to himself? If this letter was really written to me, so long as I don't open it, carrying out a Messenger's duty, I'm not really myself (a receiver), someone acting as a messenger, but instead a true Messenger. Being a true Messenger is a process filled with unending conjecture and speculation. Provided that the Messenger's mission to deliver the letter does not end in an actual delivery, but instead ends in a inexorable maze of theories and ideas, then the illusory power of language will perhaps become part of the rationality that is attributed to the text. That way all its creations will reach a shattering poetic climax.

The letter was another beginning or what is called a rebirth for human life.

"Hey!" The Messenger heard a sentimental cry coming from behind him. The young man who had taught me that I should pursue the multitudes of monks and nuns wherever they went paced through the crowds of people with an aloof idleness.

"Are you calling me?" The messenger wondered if this chance beckoning would suddenly change the direction of my journey in the Whispering City, like the way things happen in innumerable dramas—moving every soul in the audience.

No. The Messenger had already let go

of that turbulent inner apprehension. My
ever present feeling of being threatened had
been steadily increasing with the pressure
of circumstances. After this eternal, vast
narrative it had unwillingly evolved, through
a long numbing assault, into a sense of
dread. My most important mission now was
to keep waiting. The yelling of the young
monk had no particular significance.

"Judging by your puzzled expression,
I guess you still haven't found the one you
are looking for. Am I right?" His whole
demeanor revealed a calm confidence that
usually only comes from long experience,
like that of the elders among the six-fingered
people.

"It isn't important. I have some new ideas
about that."

"That's a real shame!" He continued in
the trite and torturous manner of an old
man: "New ideas may not necessarily help

you find the one you are looking for. They are only new ideas and nothing more."

The Messenger is very annoyed. How can he endure a naïve and ignorant young man gossiping on like this?

"Whether a new idea can help me or not is unimportant, what matters is that it is a new idea." I got a kick from this irrational argument. It made me think that gossiping women were very lucky.

"Now you have changed your original intentions, how come you are sticking around in the Whispering City? Didn't you come here to deliver a letter?" Although he looked perfectly relaxed, the young monk's words took on a sharper tone.

"They say that you only need to stay in the Whispering City, and sooner or later this place will become like a fantastic story. In the light of history and reality it will disappear." The Messenger thought that if one day he was in some ancient place, and because he had too many things to do he found himself doing nothing, the small and insignificant history of the six-fingered people would inevitably cheer him up. Even though the letter had infinite possibilities, what use did it have to these wild outsiders?

"But no matter what, you are a messenger!"

The letter was a tragedy with the villain acting as the hero.

"You are just provoking me with this. If I don't look like I'm doing what a messenger is supposed to do, you better make me leave."

"You have gone astray, and keep refusing to come to your senses. If you find the recipient of the letter, you will have to leave the Whispering City in the end. A person cannot remain in a dream forever."

How was it that everyone around me made offensive remarks and forced me to do things, as if they were famous sages?

The Whispering City put a spell on the Messenger. The people joined arms with ghosts; fantastic theories emerged in an endless stream. The six-fingered people truly were natural and shifting oddities. Through their constant pressing, the Messenger was close to losing his grip on reality.

"Confusion is coming." The young monk quickly retreated to a place beyond my reach. In my unclear vision he became a divine spirit of steel.

"Jesus …" I quickly reasoned that crying for help using the favorite language of the six-fingered people would be a good idea.

The Messenger hazily made out the post road full of people. They watched the Messenger jump from the beacon tower, falling through the air like a goose wing. My body was just like a letter wafting in a patch of clear brightness. I didn't hear a sound, either human or divine.

The letter was a movement.

I suddenly saw the receiver of the letter. "He isn't one of them," I said to myself.

The man's walk was very peculiar, like a dutiful son rushing home to a funeral, gloomily balking before huge waves. He continued to move about in the Messenger's lonely fantasy, peeking around, as if he was figuring out how he could escape it. His composed manner made him look almost like an umpire.

He made me feel that he was an individual of many virtues. I think if I say he looked like a fountain of virtue it would not be going too far, or that the brilliance he had in my fantasy would definitely seem too dazzling to look at the moment it entered reality. He would blind me, and leave me powerless to reach him. His silhouette blended in with the legendary dead ones. The sight seemed to the Messenger like a beautiful maiden locking eyes with her lover, their sultry love possessing the power to bury everything. He smiled at me. The Messenger saw him reveal his teeth, like breaking waves. His bright red tongue was exactly the same as the greeter's, possessing the bitterness of hard experience. I saw him moving far into the distance, at the edge of winter, his eyelids drooping. Childlike, his lingering thoughts wafted around, dropping down and then soaring again. Sea water is sky blue, so what about the coastal islands? "Those above, take care!" I heard his voice call out for the first time, soaring away from me, and then circling somewhere in the distance. Did they know what they should forget? The doomed island. It was down in the depths, under the blueness, sending its dreams back to the earth above, over and over for a thousand years. In the departure of autumn, it passed on its painful loneliness of being abandoned by the sea. "Goodnight!" he said to the broken flashes of brightness. The tide came in wave upon wave, presenting an offering of night time fossils to the sky and the coast. Sadness passed through his surging thoughts and emotions. "Take care of yourselves, take care!" he said and dipped his head under the water. "If you have something to say, whatever it is, just say it!" He tasted that endless solitude, but he was not solitude. He was a dream and solitude was blue. They looked for each other. He wanted to devote himself to it. He hung his last words on the face of a cliff, left for the silent stones as an eternal expression of condolence. As noon approached, there was a beam of sunlight. At that moment, he chose to let go of his feelings. He carried his old wounds ever southwards, so another world could heal him. He needed salt in fresh wounds. As the sea was recalling its endless journeys, sails once more entered the river flowing through his heart.

The Messenger saw the receiver take off his elegant clothes, and with an evil smile jump out of the solemn procession of time. On the streets of the Whispering City he simultaneously acted the monk and all the other parts in the charade. Then in the language of the Whispering City he told me:

"This has all been done especially for you."

To the Messenger, his honest journey had been a succession of obstacles. They made day into night. All the things he encountered led to his ultimate doom. An unoriginal and mythical fragment of history became a widespread hysteria, the fruits of fake literature, and those unhistorical statements are a failed attempt to forget the lingering,

absurd, silent and enormous shadow of the
past.

I don't know if one day the Messenger
will become an honored guest, walking
through the Whispering City. On the
uncommonly pure streets of the City, will I
have the confidence to stride along lightly
like a speck of dust, without making the wily
monks aware? As ever they are immersed
in their banal and difficult creation. As I
have everywhere, I follow the road. If the
Messenger did not carry shocking news to
fill them with despair, then he has to be
carrying good news that will make people
dance for joy. I could never have imagined
that the Messenger was temporarily and
unknowingly carrying a blank page, or
what people think is a letter.

In the course of his unconscious walk,
the Messenger's journey has moved from
a difficult to recall and bleak past, to an

unfathomable and disorienting future.

I would say that the Messenger had better quietly make his exit from the Whispering City. The Messenger can sense a disaster will strike it unexpectedly, such as being leisurely flattened in an earthquake that will be sadly described for a hundred years by later generations, and as luck would have it, allow only the worst architects to cheat death. Or, a terrible flood that will turn the City into an underwater palace overnight, leaving swathes of citizens who can't swim thrashing around in the water half-drowned. The means of the disaster has many forms in the imagination of the Messenger. All kinds of monsters and demons are incessantly bustling about within it. It really makes me think that the Messenger's letter is an intelligence report that, unfortunately, no one wants to listen to.

At the end, there is a parting scene. The monks all stand at the side of the postal road surrounding the City, saying to me in chorus:

"Maybe you ... pay attention! What we mean is ... maybe you were born in a cemetery for words. Although we don't know how you got here, you are in fact moving from one cemetery to another. Perhaps you came to the Whispering City by mistake, but the only end for you is to be buried by your mission. We say this because we are dead ones that have been put here for you."

The Messenger thought of God and the writer of the famous song. At that moment, were they drinking and doing exercises?

"Maybe!"

I have no way to escape the Messenger's ending. On a road which leads to the remote past, under the blood red setting sun, I will write another beginning:

"The letter came from an unexpected piece of writing."

Remembering
the Lady of Qin

Parting evokes the same emotion, which
varies greatly in different circumstances.

—Jiang Yan

I still remember her face, but I do not recall her name. My deceased grandma used to call her Su, which must have been her surname. Despite their age difference, grandma and Su were both intimate friends. They spent many nights together, whispering in each other's ears in the dim light, whilst knitting a hare-grey hat and a dark red scarf. She was my grandma's playmate in her twilight years. Su would comb my grandma's hair and share crispy pancakes with her. She even showed grandma her son's photo, a handsome boy who had died prematurely. She had a sense of sweetness about her, which combined with her elegance, emanated a rare soft charm. No doubt, I admired

Su tremendously, for she conjured up the epitome of the perfect woman for me. She was far different from the adults I know now. She was my mother's friend, and for reasons I could not understand at the time, lived together with us. Her arrival coincided with the season's transition from late summer to early fall. Though still in summer, the night was already pretty cold. Having a severe fever (quite usual for me at the end of every summer), I was staring up at the ceiling, feeling weak, useless and upset. Su covered my forehead with a wet towel, and hoped to distract me from the bedside pictorials and books that were better kept from the prying eyes of others. When my grandma went to the kitchen, Su told me that she had seen what I had been reading. She then paused, an indication that she understood my embarrassment and unnecessary shame. Her words ended with a meaningful gaze (yes, gaze). This was the first time that I realized how wonderful it was to speak with a woman. Her subtlety and reserve was an indisputable pleasure. Her soft intonation and clear-worded Mandarin, along with a lovely Zhejiang accent were so captivating. Su would surely laugh out loud if she read this. When I showed her my first novel, she gave me advice by asking me a question. She wanted me to consider that one might not be able to express one's feelings properly without the use of exaggeration. The naive work I showed her is nowhere to be found now, and would probably have been tossed away like a piece of garbage. But I was shocked as I came to realize how different our inner world was from what we wrote. This discovery was no big thing but had a far-reaching impact on a child like me. I kept dreaming about this difference for a long time. My dreams often featured an image of a twin bed. But why this metaphor? It used to be one of Su's favorite ways of criticizing me. She knew that I was born to be like this or perhaps realized I could never change. Her preference in literature was biased, but intriguing. She preferred direct statement, and she deemed frankness an ability rather than a trait. But for her this ability was twisted by others to become a trait. This word almost became an evil when twisted with the right tone.

We shared many common interests, but not for long. With the fever fading away, I had less time and less of a taste for reading. I was drawn to the outside world—sunlight, wind, colorful plants, bustling cities, and the joy these things invoked. Admittedly, the main culprits were my rather strange playmates. I did not know back then that I had missed out on so many things. Su left when winter came. She did not say goodbye when she was leaving. She just left me a satin-covered diary book, which was actually quite a rarity. Several pages were already ripped out. Her words were written on the last page. The writing was beautiful, like a brief postscript to a book:

Willow-trees turn green every year; yet people feel sad parting at Balin.
Parting evokes the same emotion, which varies greatly in different circumstances.

I think she might not be able to recognize me if she saw me now. My changes have even exceeded my own expectations. Her face may now bear the imprint of time, which is fair, as nobody is immune from this. I would willingly accept any changes in her look, figure or posture. Such an objective attitude was in fact taught by Su. Her demeanor and her air always conveyed the way to live an everyday life. She was like a skilled poker player, so at ease with games.

On a rainy day, Su visited us together with a stranger. My mother and grandma met her and the man at the head of the stairs. It was the first time I had seen Su, who was wearing a dark-gray nylon raincoat, and carrying an umbrella. The man's hair was wet, looking like he had just met Su. They stayed in the corridor for a while to get rid of the rain water. I would never forget her look at that moment, a woman standing in the 2-meter-wide corridor. It was raining hard outside, the corridor was dimly lit and the stair rails were damp. She raised her head all of a sudden. Her eyes were so bleak and lifeless, making her look like a patient. But there was no sadness and no trace of resentment. Such a look was not typical for the first meeting between two strangers. Maybe she read panic and confusion in my eyes. Such a face-to-face look was indifferent, but would stay in my memory forever. If we were of similar age, you might even sense a mutual avoidance. Why was that? Was it because of Su's experience and my thirst for knowledge? Now, it was my turn to be lifeless and indifferent. The gleam of exploration and fantasy in my eyes had been lost. Su once said that if memory became your daily food, you were not much different from an animal.

The door of grandma's room was closed gently behind them. Almost simultaneously came the man's weeping. He was not speaking, but just kept wailing. At that moment, I felt so lonely and helpless. That man's tears seemed meant for his messy life. Listening to such a deplorable sound while sitting on the stairs, I had the feeling that Su would speak out, based on the look in her eyes. But it was only after a long time, when the man stopped crying that Su started to talk. Her voice was low, with a comforting roughness. She was begging for forgiveness in a slow manner. I had no idea what it was about. I was playing with a deflated basketball, which slid down to the foot of the stairs.

Back then, I was in a bizarre state, with dramatic changes taking place both within and without. The grey and desperate mood was similar to that of Eugene Ionesco in his later years. I lost faith in literature and every other thing around me. Words that once gave me unparalleled delight were dead. I started to be aware of age, health, and bread-and-butter issues. The turn of seasons (I stopped using a fancier word for "turn") and change of weather were no longer poetic to me. (I told myself not to look for tempo and sound in verses and disregard rhyme.) Bigotry, temper, and contradiction were my daily symptoms. But wasn't life exactly like that? I was sure that the time of dreaming was over, and something in my spirit died. I would enter a material vacuum, comprised of a series of thriving fantasies and various cold, precise and sterile devices. For according to Ionesco—I am "immersed in the inexpressible." To be frank, I was writing a study paper on literature (I tried to finish it) with the title of *Cicada and Wing*, before I became obsessed with Su's story once again. In that paper, I attempted to conduct a parallel study on *The Aspen Papers* by Henry James and *The Gonzaga Manuscripts* by Saul Bellow. The latter was believed to be a copy of the former. A master copying another master! There was a quote from T.S. Eliot, *The Mediocre Imitates while Genius Copies*. The other group of works included *The Berlin Stories* by Isherwood and *Breakfast at Tiffany's* by Capote. Again, these two less-influential talents had to shoulder the infamy of copying each other. I wanted to discover something from this phenomenon. The laughable fact was that be it a fantasy or a symptom, I was also hoping, by searching lost precious papers or against the backdrop of turbulent times, to write a novel about a broke young writer and his house guest—a young woman. Or maybe I would write both.

Time flew by ruthlessly. My study dragged on, to no avail. I was so anxious that I went downstairs at least four to five times a day to check the mail box, or to take a stroll in the neighborhood, in the illusion that some kind of panacea was awaiting me in those stores lit by fluorescent lamps. This spirit was similar to that of Clarence when he appeared in the Madrid Rail Station—"full of gloomy vitality and lost wisdom." I could not begin or end a day's work as everything seemed so messy. It seemed that behind Bellow's orderly illustration hid an engrossing messiness. He wrote meaningfully on the first page, "… this car was running on streets of Madrid long before Clarence was born." Such a sentence was an echo of the sub-theme. It subconsciously linked Clarence's trip to Madrid with an ancient object. Ten pages later, he wrote through the words of a poet, "… the life of a poem may be longer than its theme." Another ten pages later, he described Clarence's vague thoughts, "… a lively woman maybe more worthy of pursuit than a dead poet." I hoped the relationship I had identified was a mistake.

Manuel Gonzaga, the invisible genius in the history of Spanish literature, (Clarence came for him!), talked about calcium and poems by some Spanish poet. Or like in his *Repentance*, Clarence sighed, "… ah, how we have lost everything in order to obtain everything!" (I added the exclamation, which was redundant and useless, similar to all types of praise.)

These people are all talented, and share a positive attitude towards a tragic life. Obviously they include Su, who seemed to have a natural gift for literature. You could never ignore her within a group. She was not showy, but always grabbed your attention like a ripple in a lake. Her life stories were also like that.

Her coming into my life was a little surprising for me, like an unexpected encounter. Her image, which I cared so much for, was consistent with her family and her taste. Such a feeling was hard to replicate in a photo. It was like a medium that could be penetrated by light without any trace. She passed in a flash. So the image was almost timeless, the result of days and nights and not limited to a certain date or moment. In my head, Su was made up of a series of images. There was reserve, too much reserve, while hiding her wild heart within a shell. And very clearly, there was a confidence in the reserved appearance. She just did what she wanted to do. She dressed in a stylish way, but not in contradiction with the surroundings or overly flamboyant. Put more precisely, the fabric of her clothes might seem a little out of fashion compared with the style of the day. But in those times, she saw appropriateness as an indulgence rather than an obligation. She repeatedly said that we should not confuse daytime with night. Such a notion was simple, but expressed exactly what she wanted to say.

I do not want to make you feel that I am talking about a live person. But death does no harm to her. At least in my heart it is irrelevant. I do not deny that I am rather passive in receiving this piece of news, which I did not see with my own eyes. But I give it a romantic twist. It feels like she has fallen asleep and will never wake up again. It is tiredness that has led her into an endless hibernation, like a dying snake losing a battle with consciousness.

Su's hometown was Guantao in Shandong province. But she was born in Shangdu, near Inner Mongolia. She spent the first seven years of her life on that piece of barren land, and was taken south by her uncle, who was then a merchant. I thought that was how she got her gleaming Suzhou accent. My obsession with such an accent far exceeded any attention to her early childhood. People tend to take the hint of the movement of one's family in order to paint a depressing or grand picture as a backdrop. But not me. The name of a place is compressed to a line on a map. Sometimes, the color of mountains and the location of rivers belong to a universe different from the sun, moon and stars. I think we are living in a marginal zone like Su's typical outlook, fair and clear, but sometimes a little obscure.

I could not travel back to the past. Even the intention of being close to it is deemed as an illusion. Those scenarios are still driving me forward and recalling memories. Even those coy moments are still lingering deep in my heart. It is like being slightly drunk. It all originates from my grandma's bedroom, and is aroused by a sense of fear. On the clean bed sheet that gave off a mild soapy aroma, a rich, heavy and spicy air swept by. At dusk, the lights inside the room were intoxicating. The room was filled with reflections, with windows, mirrors, and decaying walls. Su seemed rather conceited when holding a glass. She drank with grandma and chatted with her for a long time. It was not until the room was fully dark that the silhouette of Su began to approach the lamp.

Why does such an image always appear to me? What does it signify? Su and Grandma could comfort each other. The harmonious air during their get-togethers was testament to that. Such feeling aroused in my memories seemed intended to hide the vicious side of Su's life, her obscene side even in the eyes of grandma. But grandma hated that I used the word prostitute to describe her. She said it was different. She asked me to try to understand her instead of hurting her. I could not understand it. I was not old enough to have that aged sensibility. Before that I would experience and be cured of a host of mental problems, and I might even be tainted with some bad habits. All these things were awaiting me. Even in my youthful days, I vaguely felt that understanding was a luxury that only a few could afford.

I showed my first novel to her to draw her attention. My ideas were simple. I described my illusions in a clear-cut manner—a garden, a huge ancient courtyard, a place out of nowhere and with personalities hardly identifiable. I depicted scenes (which I cannot see today) and the bizarre behavior of people at dawn and late at night. I even touched upon the longing for sex in a twisting, dark and unhealthy way. In the guise of philosophy and yearning for semantic splendor, I spat out cold and pale words. In fact, my heart was like a desolate desert, the same state I am in today. Su was able to see through my mind. She was working in the kitchen while pronouncing her thoughts. I was leaning against the kitchen door, watching Su and the hot air escaping from the steamer, whilst expecting my favorite meat-filled buns. She said gently, "My little writer. You will not succeed. You are already this messy when you are so young." "Literature will justify your method, but life will not." She then pointed to her head, "You should read *The Logic of Hegel*." My father had this, but it was not on my list of must-read books. She sensed my disappointment. She approached me with a stern look and said sincerely, "Do you want to hear my stories?" Of course I wanted to and so I said yes. "You should try to identify which parts are made up," she explained. I asked, "Why do you need to make things up?"

"To help you identify which are true."

This was Su's first lesson on writing.

Mind you! It was a kind of double fabrication when I was quoting others' stories. Her words were short, like saying something was a double-sided raincoat. There was no further need to explain what that was.

Su's story was about her son's father, a southerner whose ancestors were fishermen in Fujian. He was tall and handsome, and walked with a slight limp. He did things in a hurried way, and looked exhausted whenever he smiled. The man was a chef on a boat and had just gotten divorced when he first met Su. Obviously he was very angry then. The two of them were drinking at one of Su's friends. They did not talk much but Su went with him when they left. She said, "It was so easy that I even found it bizarre. You know I had a feeling for him. I wanted to have a baby with him, which I had never felt before. But these were things that would happen later."

"Then, how did it end?" There must an ending to her story, and this was the only question I asked.

She laughed, "How could it end? Such things don't end even when you die."

"Why?"

She was still laughing, which was not the right attitude whilst reading a story.

"How should it be?" I continued asking her.

"Who?" My grandma's voice appeared from behind me. Her sudden appearance cut my conversation with Su short. Her eyes were kind but stern, as if saying that I should not try to inquire about secrets between them.

Oh, my grandma. She was so old, so kind, and way too active for a woman of her age. Such energy was not the result of a vegetarian lifestyle or exercise. It sprang from nature and instinct. Sometimes we call it 'endless youth'. Forget it. I didn't want to make up a fairy tale to justify things, that is to fabricate an old granny with tons of folk and fairy tales to tell. It was not the case. My childhood had no stove, storm lamp, rug, and wooden stool. The few stories about ghosts and men were overheard or merely hearsay. My grandma was indeed old and kind. But she did not know how to tell stories. She talked a lot in a repetitive way. When she opened her mouth, I would start running away. In retrospect, grandma was not a good story teller. More often, she preached about moral ethics. Due to her age and supreme status in my family, she was still an imposing figure despite her amiable words. She had been a widow for years and I should not pick on this elderly woman.

But she was indeed a barrier between Su and me. They shared one bedroom and were inseparable. They were intimate to such a secretive degree. I was obviously ignored not by Su, but by this invisible state of intimacy. Grandma's room became the office for outside affairs. Such a feeling was very regretful.

I still remember that man who wept in grandma's room every time he came. He was not the chef. I had never met with the father of Su's son. Back then, I was scared of tall and handsome men as their smile confused me. But this man was different. He looked too weak and thin even from a child's perspective. His finely chiseled face made him look like a scholar. He was indeed a scholar studying *I Ching*, and the *Analects*— the words and acts of Confucius now deemed to be great practical use. He buried his head in piles of papers, with several threads of hair shooting out. He started crying once parted from the dust-covered classics. A tear stained face was his signature image. I did not understand that this weak man cried over sex and love. Su explained that this kind of thing could not be said of a man. He was stubborn in his reliance on tears. Su said he cried for the sake of crying. I got some hints from their words and tried to identify their subtle meaning. Now I know that these efforts were doomed from the beginning. Su was not a bad woman, and men tended to cry for such women. I never talked with this scholar as he was always in a hurry. Of course, I don't mean to suggest that he cried all the time. For example, there was one late night—normally he would have already left by then. I woke up from bed and walked out of my room in bare feet (either because I was asked by someone to do something or I had nothing to do at all). The door of grandma's bedroom was ajar. This man, who was tortured to death by love, kneeled on the ground with tears brimming in his eyes. He was caressing Su's breasts while she was stroking his hair. I could not see her eyes. Obviously, grandma was not in the room. On such a night and at such a painful moment, people should do what they are supposed to do. They should sleep on their beds and fall deep into their dreams. I could imagine how shallow and superficial my knowledge of that night was. I even thought of myself a part of this world, an organic part. I realized how fragile my link with the world was outside my own room. Once again, I felt so alone.

It was like a festival had left and would never come back. I might expect it the following year but everything would have changed then. I seemed to have been at an excessively noisy party, only recalling the glasses and dishes but without any knowledge of what was hidden behind. Things were supposed to be a secret but in fact became an end in themselves. Su and I were two shadows, and the meaning of our subtle relationship was changed fundamentally. I hoped that she saw me from the mirror that night, as there were some things that we should both be aware of. Su must know that I was observing, conjecturing, measuring and even peeping voyeuristically on her life. But in the end I saw nothing. Su seemed totally exposed, as proven by her behavior—she was never secretive about her life. But I was blind to the whole.

I had lived in this place, this city for years. With the family moving around, I underwent a series of changes. Both sets of grandparents left the world one after another. Sorrow came and went. Houses changed and family belongings were sold. As a result, many letters and books were lost. Life was either quiet or busy, with different people coming and going. Many of them made a big fuss on the transient and simple stage of life and in the end, they all just fell. Some of them even carried a smile of accomplishment when they died. It was very admirable.

I always think that embankments have secretly changed the outlook of the city. The bund, situated adjacent to the thick river water and embellished by the sound of ripples and stained boats, was the place Su took me for a stroll. There were very few passersby on these numerous cloudy nights. Such people carried an at-ease look about them, and would stop every now and then stare into the distance. But the Shanghai they looked for was no longer there. Or maybe it had never actually existed. Because of Su and the flight of time, everything looked like a secretive part of history, continually falling, to eventually disappear one day. As her initial image was so transient, her beauty and eventual destruction had been decided from the very beginning.

That night was the most disrespectable

night. I don't want to specify exactly when it took place. What good would it do? After dinner, I had been writing in my diary on the bed, while a teacher who worked together with my mother had been playing "Arabesque" by Claude Debussy. Forget it. I should not talk about music as the music looks like a metal mesh hung with many mini bombs and always leaves me feeling scared. Su suddenly walked into mother's room and said, "She passed away." Mother was not totally unprepared for the news, but she still fainted upon seeing grandma's pale face.

I have simplified what happened that night, as it was only a setting for my grandma's passing away.

Chinese customs should not be skipped. Grandma's bedroom was soon redecorated. The teacher who was playing piano at the time acted in an orderly way, like she was there for the funeral. She helped my mother call in several thin men. They were old men dressed in light colors. They skillfully arranged the veiling, candle holders, funeral dress, and coffin. Amongst the doctors, relatives and neighbors, I saw a young man wearing glasses. He was wearing a peaked nylon cap and a short dark scarf. His face was clean shaven. Su went out of mother's room with a celadon fruit plate. She paused upon seeing him. She saw me staring at them from the end of the corridor. After a moment's hesitation, she beckoned the man into grandma's bedroom.

Mother told me that the young man was here to take a photo of grandma. He had a private photo studio nearby and once worked for a newspaper outlet. She then added that he was Su's lover and that they were together.

The whole event was like a dream. When

the noisy crowd left, the teacher was busy switching off the lamps. She then went back home. My mother was waiting for my father's call. Everything appeared over, but still it seemed that something was about to happen.

The young photographer was packing his box beside my grandma's coffin while Su was wiping grandma's body. She was delicate and slow. She bit her lips, without any trace of tiredness in her eyes.

My memory would not end here. Till now I still believe what I saw that night was an act of blasphemy, and that Su betrayed grandma's love for her. I don't know what grandma would have thought in heaven. Someone's crying had woken me up from a dream. I followed the sound to the door of grandma's bedroom. The door was open. Through layers of white drapes and against dim candlelight, I saw the most humiliating scene in my whole life. Su and her photographer were caressing each other. She threw herself onto grandma's coffin while weeping uncontrollably. The photographer was above her like her cloak. The telephone rang, and I guessed it was from my father, but Su and her lover took no notice of it. Su just kept crying. The sound might have appeared pleasing to my mother, who had no idea of what was happening. I ran to my mother's room. She had just woken up and looked exhausted. She picked up the phone with tear stained eyes.

I did not want to hide my shock. It was mixed with the impact triggered by Su's arbitrary indulgence, which was gloomy, containing both a delight and sense of failure. She exposed herself so thoroughly that nobody could hide the fact. I found it hard to paint a complete picture of her. I missed many parts of her when I faced her. For me personally, she was precious. What I admired in her was the so-called sense, which was hard for a young man to resist. It was indeed a beast. The problem was that I was not duped by it. It was like having avoided a heavy downpour. But what did it amount to in a tropical storm? It did not merely mean indulgence in sensual pleasures. I tried to justify such a thought, but to no avail. I am still confused now.

Su invited us for a lunch at a restaurant at the north of the Sassoon Mansion to thank my family. Only my mother and I went to the dinner. My late grandma had been buried a week before. Su told us that she had booked a ticket and was ready to leave. My mother kept asking her to stay but she refused. It was around two o'clock in the afternoon, and there were few customers in the restaurant.

It seemed more like an appointment for tea. Many dishes were served. But my mother and Su either kept talking to each other or were silent, watching the oil on the plates coagulate. The street outside connected to the bund. Steam whistles were heard. I did not look at my mother and I tried to avoid the eyes of Su. I just kept eating my soup. A thoughtless afternoon had made my brain empty. When the bill was asked for, Su suddenly took out cigarettes from her purse. She motioned to my mother, who refused the offer with a smile. After the lunch, Su suggested walking around the bund. My mother went back home instead, as she had a headache. Su took my hand and we walked towards the river embankment. I thought she must have been missing her son's father. I even thought about being a chef one day, but the life of separation from family was unthinkable to me.

"Where are you going?"

Su raised her hand and pointed to the river. "Who knows?" She smiled.

"If I write a book one day, where should I send it to?" I imagined there would come a day like that.

"No need." Su said. She saw that I was hurt and stopped speaking. After a while, she comforted me by saying, "If this book is very important to you, you should keep it to yourself. You shouldn't care who reads it."

A person has to read him or herself carefully. I was enlightened by Su on this. From flesh to soul, had I tried everything without fear? There would be no firm answer to that question. But I would not hide in the recesses of a book (maybe it was the journey I had to take). I saw a book unfolded, enticing and hard to resist. But I should try to avoid it. Su grasped my hands firmly. It was exactly what I needed at that moment. I could ask for nothing else.

It was obvious at that moment that my obsession with Su concealed everything. The death of my grandmother had lost some if its tragic emotion due to lust. I knew little about death. Or should I say that I mistook it as another kind of madness. I felt artificial for even talking about it, unless I was referring to the death of others, which was more about metaphysics, if not an excess of emotions.

She should have left us sooner. But she became sick after the walk. Because of a severe fever, she kept vomiting and having diarrhea all night long. My mother changed her bed sheets twice during the night. Vomit was everywhere. On the following morning, she fell unconscious. My mother locked me into my room, fearing I would be scared by the situation. I had been feeling

nervous and panicked ever since her arrival.
But I did thank my mother for doing it. I
willingly stayed in my room. I murmured
to myself while covering my head with the
sheet, in order to fend off the anxiety of
being locked up. Then I heard the sound of
footsteps. It seemed like a repeat of the night
my grandma died. Then came Su's groaning,
amid the arguments. I guessed there was a
doctor wanting to cleanse Su's blood. I was
ignorant of medicine. I did not know what
they were talking about. I prayed to myself
secretly that my softest emotion would stop
Su's suffering, as I heard the sound of a
surgical device. In fact, I was fast asleep, not
aware of what was happening outside. I was
so tired that I could not afford to consider
others' emotions.

My father came back home from Hankou
with simple luggage. He had the demeanor

of a traveler. My mother fell ill upon his arrival and her sickness continued until my father left again. I did not know what father was doing. I had no knowledge of his life, his everyday life in particular. The family thought father was a hard-working, sincere man who was used to making a living on his own. I personally thought he seemed a little afraid of marriage. Admittedly, there were few exchanges between us. We said hi to each other every time he came back and that was it. He was a silent man. There was always a tinge of stubbornness and self-indulgence in his eyes. With the flight of time, our willingness to get to know each other dissipated, and he would gradually become a stranger to me. He was like someone from another city who spoke a hard-to-understand dialect. I could not make out what he was talking about. He and mother used to be like brother and sister as they looked and acted alike. Gradually, my father became another person. His demeanor was like that of a guest. Coming home made him lose his head. He could not find his things and always bumped into chairs. He spent his time either standing beside windows in a daze, or sighing for no reason. He was very polite with mother and spoke in a proper manner, like a charity worker. His relationship with Su was rather friendly. He did not feel unhappy about mother's arrangement. He was also a filial son-in-law and would feel depressed when hearing about the last moments of grandma from Su. In less than ten days, my father had gone back to Hankou. He would come back from time to time, like a habit. He would not disappear all of a sudden as in many tragic stories. This was the first meaningful story I had been involved outside of Su's influence. It was a story about my own family and my father's image as a traveler. I still regarded it as a revelation. Marriage was just a fleeting episode in life, there to meet our inner needs. If its length was equivalent to life, it would leave people speechless

In those days, I was busy taking care of these two ailing women. I heated water, distributed pills, went to the pharmacy and the cigarette shop. On the way I would visit my friends. But they all gave me a strange look, like I had brought bad omens. Both mother and Su were very fragile. Partly due to the medication, they would doze off and wake up repeatedly. I seemed to provide the proof that they were still alive. To me they seemed like ghosts. Sometimes mother and Su would extend their hands to me, which were similarly soft, pale and damp in the center. What had brought these two women together? They were like two women late in life, with frighteningly sparse hair scattered on their pillows. They would ask me similar questions, probably to relieve my anxiety. They made me feel distanced from the outside world and they became the sole link between me and the world. But those days were the most colorful days of my life. They were like a symbol that equipped me with the capacity to identify madness. I could pin down those who acted like fools. I started to know what was good and what was bad. I started categorizing people into groups, half of them belonging in a mad house. I knew this idea was crazy but it fitted the state in my home back then. I wanted to stop or make a transition, as in a novel, towards either open land or towards an even narrower and darker road. Would that passage always await me like the abyss of lust and friendship, without any tempering by illusions and words?

Su started to recover and her state became much better than my mother's. Then, the scholar and the photographer took turns coming to our home. There were some other men who acted like doctors or guests, behaving in an objective, calm and composed way. They were from all ranks of society, and their way of speaking and behavior varied greatly. All in all there were a dozen of them. Generally speaking, those men were all quite polite. They would only stay a while beside Su's bed. Sometimes they would chat with each other for a while, light a cigarette in the corridor, and brush away the invisible dust on their hats. They looked like total strangers with a ridiculous attention to detail. I was charged with receiving and sending them off. So, I kept in mind who they were, and then told my mother about their visits, like they would be

of a comfort to her. On the other hand, I did
not want Su to recover soon as I preferred it
better when she lay in bed. I would be lost
in the moment when I approached her bed
and looked at her. Such a feeling would not
disappear easily, but would need constant
nursing and nurturing. Su seemed more
than willing to accept my naive obsession
and emotional devotion. Back then, her
smile was agreeable, giving her a glowing
appearance.

One day in autumn, someone sent a big
bouquet of roses to Su through a student-
looking girl on a tricycle. Su seemed very
happy. She carefully put the roses in a vase,
and then came to my room and said to me
secretively, "I am going to meet a friend. But
I need a companion."

"Is it far?" The notion of a companion
made my thoughts race.

"It's less than a half-hour walk." I was a little disappointed, but my imagined trip was not much longer. It was just a feeling that needed to be justified by a trip. I took out my leather shoes and brushed them so many times that they looked rather oily. I was hoping to discuss literature with her on the way, as this topic had been ignored by us for a long time. Su walked out of the room after getting dressed. She wore a dark-colored striped light woolen coat, which might not have been the right choice for the season, but suited her post-recovery look well.

We gave up the plan to walk as it was too windy. Su wanted to take a tram, so we crossed a narrow alley and arrived at a street to the east. Su shivered a little in the strong wind. There were few people waiting for the bus. A newsboy passed us. Su offered her hand to me upon getting on the bus, saying,

"Mind your shoes."

When the sky darkened, Su took me to a grey building. The trip took more than half an hour. We didn't talk about literature. She seemed to have a fever as her face was pale. I just followed her without knowing where we were going.

We travelled to the third floor by elevator. Su knocked on a brown wooden door. A maid received us, and upon seeing Su let us in. What happened next was sad. A drunken man was lying on a sofa in a big room at the end. The room smelled of mildew and was messy. For some reason, the maid was wiping the man's body down with alcohol. He was like a corpse, allowing the maid to move him. His pants were pulled off, exposing his ugly and pale bottom. The blanket used to cover him slipped onto the floor. Su, deeply upset, bent down to pick it up, asking the maid to fetch a bowl of hot water. Then, she sat on the side of the sofa and held the alcoholic's head in her arms.

I would never understand why this man ended up in Su's arms, but I could never get an answer from Su. She was a rather secretive woman. My mother once warned me of this, the warning sounding like a summary of Su's life. She had never known what she wanted.

How could that be? In my eyes, Su always chose the same type of men. They idled around and were very lazy. They had nothing to do, but always looked anxious. They always had a pitiful look. I did not despise them. Whenever Su appeared, they would without exception behave rather desperately, like a beggar on a winter's night, so impoverished and down. They were all incurable.

This vermin-like man sobered up after Su's care. "The party, the party." He opened his eyes and tried to describe the venue. He said, "It is luxurious!" Su looked at him with tender love and answered his ravings. Shattered vessels were scattered around. I tried to link the situation with the metaphor of blood-red roses, which was not hard to do. Su's soft words were her petals of logic. (I was close to reaching the same conclusion as Su did about Hegel.) "Are you hungry?" Oh, she was worried that he might be hungry, not that he would drown himself in alcohol. These types of people were always accompanied by the opium poppy. They grabbed life through an opium pipe. They captivated Su's forehead and lip with the gentle look in their eyes. The man's ultra-thin silhouette carried the innocent bearing of a virgin. Men like him were fatally attractive to Su. All of a sudden, the man started cursing Su, and kept shivering like a malaria patient, which was apparently also Su's affliction. But this was also a sort of arrogance, as he abused Su to stay sober and to hurt her. Su was silent, not gloomy at all. Her eyes were filled with tears. Then he started tossing things, lifting chairs, throwing bottles outside the window, and waiting for the sound of their smashing. He pounced on Su with clenched teeth, shoved and pushed her. Outside dawn had already broken.

I was too small to face such violence. Su took me to the room next door and ordered me to sleep and keep silent. But I felt shattered. I didn't hold any resentment in my eyes as there was no such feeling in Su's pure eyes.

He fainted, partly due to the lack of alcohol. He fell down like a corpse. The big bang stirred my ears. I thought Su would return to him again, and kiss him. I was well aware of that.

Who are more ignorant, those from desolate regions or those obsessed with books? On those nights I spent alone walking on streets, Su's image always appeared in my mind. What my eyes saw formed a true reading, naked, greedy, and soaked in lust. The striking part was that there was no image for me to appreciate when I quieted down, not even an image of court official or clown.

On the same day, I was invited to dinner with the alcoholic during one of his sober moments. Wearing a suit too big for him, he took me to the destination. On the way, he would stop to light a cigarette or pick his nose. He had a rather flamboyant demeanor. From the back, he seemed like an energetic man without any bad habits, given that he was not at that moment soaked in alcohol. When I was following him I did not realize however that he was in fact heading to a pub.

He first went to an apartment to claim some debts. Before entering, he turned back and asked me, "How do I look?"

I was honest with my answer, "You haven't shaved."

He felt his chin and said, "Well, it does not matter. Wait for me at the entrance of Gongdelin. Those who owe me money don't like kids."

"I am not a kid," adding, "and I don't like vegetarian food."

"I don't like vegetarian food either. But go there and wait for me." He went into the apartment but returned right away, "I can take you to theatre to make up for things."

I thought he was a considerate alcoholic.

In retrospect, I remembered it was a long time before the alcoholic returned. In fact, it was night when he walked out of the building carrying a big leather case. By this time, he looked more like the alcoholic he had always been. He carried a case and stumbled towards me.

"Come and help me." He yapped, "This stupid thing is fucking heavy. I could not hold it without drinking a little."

I helped him with the case, which was not heavy as it was not fully packed. I thought he was just too weak to hold it. We took the case and went to a restaurant decorated with lanterns. We looked like two cargo carriers.

The case and objects inside it were all guarantees. He took me to a street side table. The case was put on a chair. It drew a lot of attention as it was much taller than the table, looking like a fence.

He ordered whisky, which was something new to me. He said modestly, "You should drink a little. I am not against kids drinking."

"No, thanks," I refused.

He looked a little regretful. When the whisky had been poured, he started to tell me how he had demanded the payment of the debt, "That guy told me he had no money. But I was considerate. He even drinks more than me. In the end, he gave me a case and asked me to take whatever garments I wanted. Do you want to see them?" He was about to open the case in the public. I said no again.

"Fine. Let's just focus on drinking."

"You, not us," I corrected him.

"What difference does it make? There is no you and me in drinking." He was soon drunk. I accepted his offer of dinner but did not eat anything. In the end, I called Su, who came to pay the bill and take us home.

Su asked me, "Whose case is this?"

"I don't know. I stayed outside. I didn't see that man. But he was just another alcoholic." I was telling the truth, only in an edited manner. The case was left in the restaurant. He didn't remember it when he was sober again. Memory was a luxury he could not afford in his life.

This was the woman whose origin and background I had no idea of, and my interest in her was not about particulars. A series of names and the existence of several men did not convey any definite information. It was like Sally written by Isherwood, "all charm was centered on the last postcard." It was like one of Capote's stories, on which "full of deep emotion" was written. The handwriting was of a woman that had disappeared from the author's vision.

"You are her son?" A middle-aged man asked.

"No."

Without further explanation, he murmured to himself, "Then you must be her brother. No, that cannot be. She told me she has no brothers. Or is she lying to me?"

He was exactly the man who Su had described to me; the movie actor.

I told him the truth, "Su and my mother went to church."

"But today is not Sunday." The actor seemed rather proud of his intelligence.

"They went to meet a friend."

"A woman?" He was really a soft-spoken man.

"A man." I made this up. It was effective as he started pacing peevishly. Anxiety, suspicion and jealousy took turns emerging on his face, not necessarily in this order.

He pointed his hand towards me and asked, "You! Do you know what that man does?" He was afraid that I did not get his meaning and began posing as boss, office worker, player, teacher and other typical professions. I kept shaking my head, indicating denial or failure to understand. I had watched many movies featuring him. He mostly had merely one line or else no lines at all. He was once famous for acting in a love story. In that movie, he was a lazy husband who never washed his feet. That character would refuse to put his feet in water even if his wife placed a basin in front of him. Instead, he scrubbed his feet together above the basin, so-called dry washing. So, he did enjoy a certain level of fame for a short period, as that movie had marked the peak of his career. Now, he stood wearing a shiny pair of shoes, his pacing around reflecting his anxious mood.

I knew of his scandalous affairs, but it was difficult to picture him together with Su. I would feel drowned in depression whenever I pictured Su alone. This once-famous comedian was now just another clown. He was indeed handsome, but he always squeezed his face into various bizarre expressions. He took pride in making others laugh. This man won Su's love, and her lack of decisiveness before going to the church was an exception to her otherwise reserved composure.

When they were together, they did not refrain from showing their love for each other. Like in a movie, the two of them hugged and kissed without reservation. My mother and I were like two moviegoers watching a free movie. This actor was frank with his life. I guessed his attitude won Su's heart over. His Mandarin had a strong southern accent, which was suitable in expressing his love for a woman. He was a fervent fan of Geoffrey Chaucer. He got inspiration and a clear attitude towards life from The Canterbury Tales. I guessed that he was one of those whom Su talked to about literature.

He would say, "Geoffrey's tales always begin with an interesting depiction of warriors. I love that picture—a bearded warrior wearing a scarf, riding a horse with a big smile on this face. There is a small knife on his belt, shiny under the sunlight of medieval times." He would shift the topic all of sudden, "How charming was sunlight back then!" He would stumble a little at that moment. He said he always took several pairs of glasses for the convenience of reading scripts, protecting himself from sand, looking at the entrance of night clubs from a distance, and sitting alone dispiritedly in a darkened cinema.

On his wedding night (according to his vivid accounts), he declared himself to be a warrior. He said that his wife found the term highly meaningful on the matrimonial bed as it contained a certain humble modesty, a teasing and free quality, as well as bravery, flexibility and seamlessness. His wife would gradually understand all parts of the meaning. His life after marriage was both healthy and happy, with little trouble, until the day he met Su.

He then declared at the table, "I am going to get a divorce." He sounded like he was liberating himself. But Su just kept smiling without talking. She looked at him with a broad smile, as if appreciating a movie.

He was obviously the most pleasant table guest I had had. I could not ignore that, despite my prejudice against him. In addition, I was also biased towards Su. Therefore, Su's attachment to him dominated everything, including my attitude to the world.

Su and my mother were quiet and calm in the days before her departure. There had been few visits to our home, except for some bouquets of flowers sent to Su. Life seemed as if suspended. Su left silently, not out of any effort to avoid me but (which I believed strongly) because of a desire to simply forget. It was not necessary to prepare an occasion to say goodbye to me. Otherwise we would talk about literature again for no reason, which was rather embarrassing. My mother could tolerate my daily absent-mindedness, but she was hesitant about special occasions, as she did not know what strange things I would do. I did not want to upset her.

Su left. I have not seen her since her departure. Those people who appeared in my life because of Su also disappeared. I heard fragments of news about her years later. She still lived in this city, sometimes here, sometimes there. But she moved a lot. She lived with that actor for a period of time. They had a daughter, but Su deserted her daughter and the actor in the end. I was convinced that she would not have had a child with that man if she had not loved him. I did not know where this idea came from, maybe a look, a gesture, a walk, or the dreary tone in her accent. All in all, the idea always jumped in my head and lingered there. My mother seldom mentioned Su after she left. She seemed to regard Su as just a guest, nothing more. Mother would allude to her when remembering grandma. To a certain extent, Su did move out of our life together with grandma's death.

Since then, new things have emerged in my life: whisky, cigarettes, cameras, classic literature, delicacy and an endless love for movies. A stranger might conclude what kind of person I was based on these things, plus the background of the old times.

I even wrote some short stories, to the chagrin of my mother. She regarded such writing as boring, vulgar, shallow, and ignorant. I wanted to know why she called me ignorant. I was fine with the other accusations as life was extremely boring in itself.

But my mother's comments on my work ended there. Maybe in her eyes, ignorance was not something to be dwelled upon. You may be ignorant in one field, meaning you will be ignorant forever. Like the popular concept of synchronicity. Ignorance has no beginning and no end, and will not change due to emergence of new things. It is different from those well-informed about life. Forget it, I will stop categorizing. I do not want to pretend to be a supporter of structuralism as it does not matter at all. What's more important is whether you pretend to be so. I guess my mother's definition of ignorance might contain this meaning.

One day (fake? No. I don't remember the exact date but I still remember the location), I met a woman. There was something about her that sparked my memory. I imagined her to be the daughter of Su and the actor. Her face did have the lonely look of someone deserted since birth. She sat in a corner of a room, like a woman who would give everything to guard her moral integrity. A drunken man with a glass approached her, demanding to drink with her. He put his face close to her ears and said, "Who are you preserving your virginity for?" Then he staggered away.

"He must be drunk," I explained to her, covering my embarrassment about overhearing their conversation.

"I hope you are not drunk." She maintained her composure.

"No, definitely not," I said to myself. I made another sip to moisten my throat so that I would not choke. "I want to ask you about a person. I think you might know her. But, please do not avoid my question."

"Go ahead."

"Cheers!" A toast to begin the conversation. "Has your mother left you? She must have deserted you and your father."

"Is this a game or joke? If so it isn't funny."

"Please answer me!" I had to take another sip as I needed to build the courage to continue.

"If yes is the answer you are looking for, then the answer is yes."

"Yes!" I heard a yes. I sat beside her and said, "Ok, let's talk about your mother. How is she?"

"Yeah," she seemed to try to recollect the past or struggle to choose the right word, "she has always, always been lonely."

"Undoubtedly." I encouraged her, "Cheers!"

The man that staggered away came back to listen to our conversation.

"She has been living on her own."

"That's exactly how she is," I thought I should comment every now and then.

"She loves my father and me very much."

"What does she do?" The man cut in.

"Right, what does she do?" I had been asking myself this question for years.

"She does everything or nothing at all."

"Why?" The man asked.

"Why what? Why does she have to do something? What is there to be done?"

Many people were being drawn to us, "Right, what should be done?" They were asking each other. The floor gave a cracking sound. Some chairs were moved. People started to drink together, with a mumbling sound from their throats, as if they were gargling.

"She is not well. She is old." Everyone sighed. This was not in doubt.

"Let's go dancing." Someone proposed.

The crowd dispersed. "Who is young?" The drunken man asked before he left. He did not wait for the answer.

"Anything else?" Now we were left on our own.

"What else do you want to know?" She was still calm, like she was the person controlling the game.

"Nothing else." The conversation ended abruptly. I did not know what I wanted to know. "Thank you. Cheers!"

"Cheers!" She looked at the wine inside the glass and finished it off.

"Ok. Let's talk about you. How have you and your father been since your mother left?"

She said I should refrain from listening to her story. She gripped my arm firmly. That was days later. Mother went downstairs to see a guest off. We were drinking warm tea inside the room. It was so quiet that the quietness itself became a sound. We were speechless, with our fingers intertwining. The hammer-shaped earrings dangling on her ears were flashy. Something was disappearing in her profile and neck covered by her long hair, like a village hidden behind green trees. I followed my habit of old (like I once did) and looked at her closely. Her smile seemed to have an apologetic air, something I was familiar with. No one was more absent-minded than us. I did not notice things we loved, or just was too hesitant to approach them. Sometimes I closed my eyes, feeling that I was so lucky—surviving through wars with only minor injuries. Now amid groups of strangers, I gazed to uncover the happiness hidden in their tortured bodies.

I came close to her face and profile and saw a slight panic, like I was about to intrude on an irregular life. She breathed heavily when she was asleep or pretending to be asleep. I would be woken up by this sound and fail to get back to sleep again. This was personally incomprehensible

Mother came back and entered my room. She gave me an inquisitive look, but did not get an answer.

She smiled at my mother politely. We continued sipping tea. At this moment, I saw myself removed from past. My mourning ceremony ended. All equipment was moved away and all lights were switched off. The murky picture deep in the abyss disappeared completely. We got up and went out in to the street. We were immediately drowned by the crowds.

Nobody could see this side of life as it existed on a missed page. What we were able to read were only parts that could not be pieced together. They were then compiled into books, like our lives were just a collection of loose-leaf pages.

"If I wrote a book one day …"

I heard myself saying something said before.

Su said, "I would not read it."

I once thought about using a simple word to describe Su, to sum up her life. I thought of a cat, without any implied meaning, as I also alluded to the rats she used to pursue. If every sentence is a symbol, Su would not have the capacity to burden it. For a woman like her, an abstract would cover all her affairs. Su's life had been too short and seems further and further away from me. The alcohol, the sharp laughter, the unrestricted lust, and the ordinary and bizarre faces of her lovers have vanished from my mind. So have the old times, which together with boys and compradors, the colors and original decorations of buildings, the pidgin English, soap ads broadcast in private radio

stations, movies and theatres, the ringing
of streetcars, and anecdotes, have now
become the focus of my remembrance. At
the heart of it is Su, passionate but unknown
to others. It is private and secret. It is lost
in oblivion and is a way of self-expansion.
Increasingly it becomes a view in the mirror,
cold, blurred, and unimportant. There is no
commitment in her story. If you feel bad
about it, the feeling will accompany you
forever. She is like the scorching hot but
desolate desert, totally exposed. It is distant
but close, without any sense of metaphysics.
But I am completely captivated by it, like the
way other objects seem to other people.

Stories by Contemporary Writers from Shanghai